Tiddalick the Greedy Frog

An Aboriginal Dreamtime Story

Lee Aucoin, *Creative Director*
Jamey Acosta, *Senior Editor*
Heidi Fiedler, *Editor*
Produced and designed by
Denise Ryan & Associates
Illustration © Nina Rycroft
Rachelle Cracchiolo, *Publisher*

Teacher Created Materials
5301 Oceanus Drive
Huntington Beach, CA 92649-1030
http://www.tcmpub.com
Paperback: ISBN: 978-1-4333-5636-0
Library Binding: ISBN: 978-1-4807-1735-0
© 2014 Teacher Created Materials
Printed in China
Nordica.072018.CA21800726

Retold by
Nicholas Wu

Illustrated by
Nina Rycroft

Contents

The Aboriginal people of Australia tell stories about a mystical time known as Dreamtime. These stories help them remember old ways and explain mysterious events. They tell of ancient spirits that came to Earth. These spirits created plants, animals, and landmarks. The tale of Tiddalick is one of these old stories. It is treasured by people around the world.

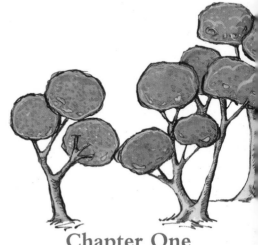

Chapter One

Dreamtime

Once, there were no mountains, no rivers, no animals, and no people. There was no sun, no rain, and no wind. There was only darkness.

Then, the Dreamtime came to be, and wonderful things began to happen. The Rainbow Serpent came down from the sky and slithered across the Earth. Mountains rose, and valleys appeared. Rivers flowed, and the Earth was slowly covered with trees, plants, and flowers. Animals appeared as if they had been blown in by the wind.

In those days, when the Earth was green and beautiful, there lived a giant frog named Tiddalick. He was bigger than the rocks. He was bigger than the trees. He was even bigger than the mountains.

When Tiddalick was happy, everything was calm and peaceful. When he was grumpy, the Earth would tremble, rocks would fall, and winds would rage.

Chapter Two

The Greedy Frog

One morning, Tiddalick woke up in
a very grumpy, greedy mood. He was so
grumpy and greedy that when he went down
to the lake to drink, he drank and drank
until he had drunk all the water in the lake.

Then, he went down to the river. He drank and drank until he had drunk all the water in the river. Tiddalick was so greedy that he kept drinking night and day. He drank all the water from the lakes and streams. The greedy frog drank so much that there wasn't a drop of water left in the whole world. Tiddalick was so full, he could hardly move. All he could do was lie down, close his great yellow eyes, and go to sleep.

The land dried out and cracked. The rivers turned to dust. The trees lost their leaves. The flowers did not bloom. Animals began to die. Nothing moved, and there was no sound. There was no rain. The land suffered from a terrible drought.

The animals cried, "We have nothing to drink. We have nothing to eat. There is no rain and no water. What can we do?"

Chapter Three

The challenge

Wise old Wombat said, "We need to talk with Tiddalick. We can ask him to give us back our water."

So one by one, the animals went to Tiddalick. The animals argued about who should approach him first.

Kangaroo was bravest. He said, "I will speak with him."

"Tiddalick," he cried, "I am the jumping kangaroo. I cannot jump anymore because I am so weak. All I can do is lie in the dust of the dry riverbed. Please, give us back our water."

Then Dingo said, "I am the wild dog who barks and howls in the night. I cannot bark and howl anymore because I am so weak. All I can do is lie in the dust of the dry riverbed. Please, give us back our water."

Kookaburra came next. He said, "I am the bird who laughs in the trees. I cannot laugh anymore because I am so weak. All I can do is perch on a branch of a dead tree. Please, give us back our water."

Then, Cockatoo squawked loudly. "I am the bird with the brilliant white feathers and a bright yellow crest. I am very, very weak. My beautiful yellow crest is growing pale. Please, give us back our water."

Tiddalick did not stir. He didn't even open one of his big yellow eyes. It seemed that the greedy, grumpy frog would be the only one to survive.

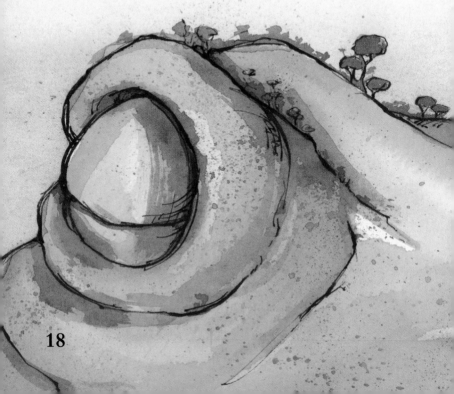

Chapter Four

A Solution

The animals were about to give up. It seemed they would die in the dust. But then, they heard a small voice say, "I have an idea."

The animals looked around. There was little Bandicoot, flapping his big rat ears. "If we could make Tiddalick laugh, I'm sure the water would flow from his mouth," Bandicoot squeaked. "Maybe we can tickle him. Let's find a branch."

So, the animals struggled to their feet and gathered around the giant frog to see if they could make him laugh. First, they tried tickling him. But Tiddalick didn't seem impressed.

Kookaburra told some of his funny stories. Everyone laughed and laughed, but Tiddalick didn't. He didn't even blink.

Next, Kangaroo and Emu jumped up and down, and around and around. Everyone laughed and laughed, but Tiddalick didn't. He didn't even open one eye!

Lizard came down from a tree. He opened his frill and showed the animals his bright orange and red scales. Then, he ran around and around on his hind legs. Everyone laughed and laughed, but Tiddalick didn't. He didn't even stir.

"Come on, Tiddalick! Laugh, you big, squelchy frog. If you could see yourself, you would laugh until you cried," the animals said.

But all seemed lost. The animals were sure they were doomed. Tiddalick would never laugh. And they would never have water again.

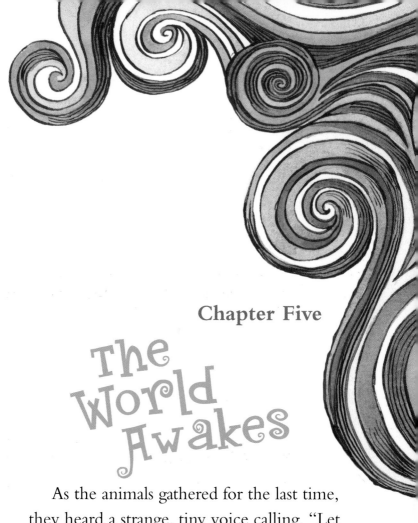

Chapter Five

The World Awakes

As the animals gathered for the last time, they heard a strange, tiny voice calling, "Let me try! Let me try to make him laugh."

It was Eel, who had slithered up from a
dry billabong. He began to dance. First,
he moved slowly, but soon he danced faster
and faster. He wriggled, twisted, and
turned himself into strange shapes. Then, he
jumped onto Tiddalick's tummy, spinning
around like a tornado.

Tiddalick began to shiver.

Tiddalick began to quiver.

Tiddalick began to giggle.

Tiddalick's giggle became a gurgle.

Tiddalick's gurgle became louder and
louder until the Earth trembled.

Then, all of a sudden, he began to laugh.
The animals ran for shelter as water gushed
out of his mouth like a huge waterfall.
Tiddalick laughed until every drop of water
was out of his stomach.

29

The water filled the lakes, the ponds, the billabongs, and the swamps. It filled the waterholes and the rivers.

New life came to the Earth. The whole world woke as if from a deep sleep. Trees grew and flowers bloomed. Animals wandered through the grasses. Birds flitted from tree to tree. Slowly, the Earth became beautiful again. And Tiddalick became just a little frog.

And, to this day, the Aboriginal people of Australia know that when they see little frogs filling themselves up with water and burying themselves in the ground, there will soon be a drought.

Nicholas Wu lives in Korumburra, Australia. He loved reading the story of Tiddalick when he was young and was delighted to find that it was originally told by the Gunai, the Aboriginal people who lived where the town of Korumburra now stands. Nicholas also wrote *The Bear's Story by Baldwin B. Bear* for Read! Explore! Imagine! Fiction Readers.

Nina Rycroft grew up in Australia and now lives in Auckland, New Zealand. She studied graphic design in Sydney and worked in Sydney and London before becoming an illustrator. The first picture book Nina illustrated, *Little Platypus,* received a Children's Book Council of Australia Notable Book award. Since then, Nina has illustrated many children's books, including *Ballroom Bonanza,* which was a finalist in the CJ Picture Book Awards International Competition. *Tiddalick the Greedy Frog* is Nina's first book for Read! Explore! Imagine! Fiction Readers.